cloverleaf books™

Fall and Winter Holidays

Grace's Thanksgiving

Lisa Bullard

illustrated by **Katie Saunders**

Ⅿ MILLBROOK PRESS · MINNEAPOLIS

For Sam —L.B.
For Evie, Neve, Alfie, and Archie
   (friends forever) —K.S.

Millbrook Press
A division of Lerner Publishing Group, Inc.
241 First Avenue North
Minneapolis, MN 55401 U.S.A.

Website address: www.lernerbooks.com

Main body text set in Slappy Inline 18/28.
Typeface provided by T26.

Library of Congress Cataloging-in-Publication Data

Bullard, Lisa.
    Grace's Thanksgiving / by Lisa Bullard ; illustrated by Katie
Saunders.
        p.   cm. — (Cloverleaf books™—fall and winter holidays)
    Includes index.
    ISBN 978-0-7613-5076-7 (lib. bdg. : alk. paper)
    ISBN 978-1-4677-0122-8 (eBook)
    1. Thanksgiving Day—Juvenile literature. I. Saunders, Katie,
ill. II. Title.
GT4975.B85 2013
394.2649—dc23   2011048493

Manufactured in the United States of America
2 – BP – 2/1/13

TABLE OF CONTENTS

Chapter One
Turkey Day

Gobble, gobble. Can you guess what today is? It's **Thanksgiving!**

Dad calls it **Turkey Day.** Mom says it's a holiday for **giving thanks.**

Thanksgiving is the fourth Thursday of November in the United States. Many other countries have different days of thanks.

This year, I'm making a **"Thankful List."**
I'm thankful for the good Thanksgiving smells.

6

Food is a big part of Thanksgiving. Many people eat turkey. They may have stuffing, gravy, and cranberries too. Some people also serve meals to those who don't have enough to eat.

I'm thankful Dad bought such a **big turkey!**

I'm always thankful for dessert. I'm usually glad for my dog, Zadie.

Pies are a popular Thanksgiving dessert. This includes pumpkin pie, apple pie, and pecan pie. Pumpkins, apples, and pecans all grow in the United States. They become ripe in the fall.

Today I'm glad for something else. I stopped Zadie before she ate all our **Thanksgiving pies!**

Chapter Two

Fill Up with Family

Grandpa snuck some pie too. But I'm thankful he's here anyway! I'm happy we have lots of **family** visiting.

Many people travel to see family for Thanksgiving. Some fly or drive long distances. It's one of the busiest travel times of the year.

Mom says Thanksgiving fills us with love and turkey.

I watch the **Thanksgiving parade** with my little brother.

Many different places have Thanksgiving parades. The most famous is the Macy's Thanksgiving Day Parade. It's in New York City. It features giant balloons.

I'm thankful for him even though he bugs me sometimes.

Chapter Three

Why We Have Thanksgiving

On TV, they talk about the **first Thanksgiving.** The people we call the **Pilgrims** were new to America.

In 1621, they had a three-day feast. They were celebrating good crops. Nearby **Native Americans** helped with these crops. They joined the feast too.

Native Americans and these newcomers didn't continue to get along. War started in 1675. Thanksgiving is a sad day for some Native Americans. It reminds them of bad times.

Mom says this feast did happen. But it wasn't really the first Thanksgiving.

Yam Festival
(West Africa)

Cerealia
(ancient Rome)

Sukkot
(Jewish people)

People have always had days of thanks. They thank their god or gods. People also have **harvest feasts** around the world.

Chuseok (Korea)

Thanksgiving was held in America at times between 1621 and 1863. But it was only in certain years. Or it happened only in some places. Sometimes it was on different days in different places.

Thai Pongal (Tamil people)

Crop Over (Barbados)

Mom says I should be thankful for **Sarah Josepha Hale.** She worked to make Thanksgiving a yearly holiday for the whole country.

Sarah Josepha Hale also wrote "Mary Had a Little Lamb."

Finally, **President Abraham Lincoln** agreed. He made Thanksgiving a **national holiday** in 1863.

Chapter Four

Time to Eat!

It's time to eat! We hold hands and say **grace**. That means we thank God for the food.

I add one more thing to my list. I'm thankful I have a
Thanksgiving name. Didn't I tell you? My name is **Grace!**

Make Your Own Turkey Cookies

You can help get ready for your family's Thanksgiving feast by decorating these turkey cookies!

What you will need:

Prebaked round sugar cookies
Orange frosting
Candy corn
M&M's

Toothpicks
Butter knife
Waxed paper

How to decorate your turkey cookies:

1) Study the picture on this page. It will help you as you decorate!

2) Set your cookies on the waxed paper.

3) Use the butter knife to spread frosting along the top edge of your cookie.

4) Place candy corn all along this frosted edge. The points of the candy corn should be facing down. This will be your turkey's tail feathers.

5) Use a toothpick to make two frosting dots on your turkey. Put them where the eyes would be.

6) Stick two M&M's on top of these frosting dots to make the eyes.

7) Add a tiny frosting dot on top of the M&M's too.

8) Use a toothpick and the frosting to draw two feet and a beak on your turkey.

9) Eat!

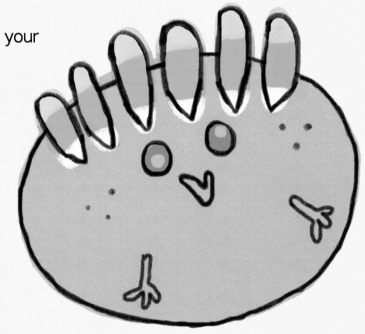

GLOSSARY

celebrating: doing something to show how special or important something is

Cerealia (SEER-ee-AIL-yuh): a long-ago harvest feast in Rome (in modern-day Italy)

crops: plants that are usually grown for food

Chuseok (CHOO-sock): a harvest feast in Korea

gobble: the noise made by a male turkey

crop over: a harvest feast on the Caribbean island of Barbados

grace: a prayer said at a meal

harvest: a time when vegetables, fruits, or grains are ripe and ready to eat

Jewish: related to the religion called Judaism or to the people known as Jews

Native Americans: the first people to live in America

Pilgrims: a name later given to a group of people from England who arrived in America in 1620 and settled at Plymouth Bay in Massachusetts

ripe: ready to be picked and eaten

stuffing: a food made out of bread and other things mixed together and cooked inside a turkey. Dressing is similar but is cooked in a pan.

Sukkot (soo-COAT): a harvest feast celebrated by Jewish people

Tamil (TAH-muhl): related to a group of people who speak the Tamil language. The language is spoken in parts of India and Sri Lanka.

Thai Pongal (TIE PAHNG-guhl): a harvest feast celebrated by Tamil people

thankful: glad or grateful

yam festival: a harvest feast in parts of West Africa

BOOKS

Heiligman, Deborah. *Celebrate Thanksgiving with Turkey, Family, and Counting Blessings.* Washington, DC: National Geographic, 2006. Read this book to learn more about the ways we celebrate Thanksgiving and the history behind the holiday.

Rustad, Martha. *Fall Harvests: Bringing in Food.* Minneapolis: Millbrook Press, 2011. Learn about how foods are grown and then harvested in the fall.

Sloate, Susan. *Pardon That Turkey: How Thanksgiving Became a Holiday.* New York: Penguin, 2010. Find out more about Sarah Josepha Hale and how she helped make Thanksgiving a national holiday.

WEBSITES

Just for Kids
http://www.plimoth.org/learn/just-kids
You will find lots of great Thanksgiving activities at this website from the Plimoth Plantation. You can talk like a Pilgrim, find recipes and coloring pictures, and learn more about the Native Americans who came to the 1621 feast.

Kids Jokes—You Quack Me Up!!! Thanksgiving Jokes
http://www.ducksters.com/jokesforkids/thanksgiving.php
Check out the funny Thanksgiving jokes at this website.

November Rad Road Trips Passport
http://www.radroadtrips.com/wp-content/uploads/RRTNov2009TripPassport.pdf
Are you traveling by car for Thanksgiving? Print out this activity book from Rad Road Trips. It has many different activities for you and others for your family.

LERNER *e* SOURCE™
Expand learning beyond the printed book. Download free, complementary educational resources for this book from our website, www.lernerresource.com.